THE CAT THAT CLIMBED THE CHRISTMAS TREE

By Susanne Santoro Whayne
Illustrated by Christopher Santoro

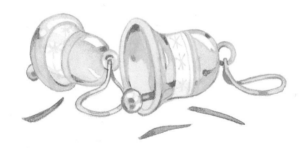

A GOLDEN BOOK • NEW YORK
Western Publishing Company, Inc., Racine, Wisconsin 53404

It was Benny the cat's first Christmas. On Christmas Eve armloads of boxes were carried into the living room. Out of the tissue paper and cellophane bags, wonderful objects appeared to be hung on the Christmas tree.

Benny was fascinated. He stood on his hind legs and grabbed the lowest branch of the tree with an eager paw.

"Now, Benny, behave yourself!" Emily laughed and swooped him away. "Christmas trees are not for cats!"

But after the family was in bed, Benny sat at the foot of the Christmas tree. Glass balls sparkled in the moonlight. Tiny sleds, velvet mice, and reindeer with real bells dangled from branch tips. In the upper boughs, Chinese ladies and miniature soldiers floated in the half shadows. And on the highest branch, an angel stood in silent watch.

Benny just had to have a closer look. His muscles tensed, and his tail twitched. What a climb this would be—right to the very top!

In one quick leap he was on a low branch,
nose to nose with an old, fuzzy reindeer. He
gave a little tap to make the reindeer spin
and, for good measure, a playful growl.

The reindeer tossed his head and snorted.

Benny was so surprised, he nearly fell off the
branch. "You're real!" he said.

"Of course," the reindeer replied. Then Benny
heard excited chatter and bits of song filtering
through the branches.

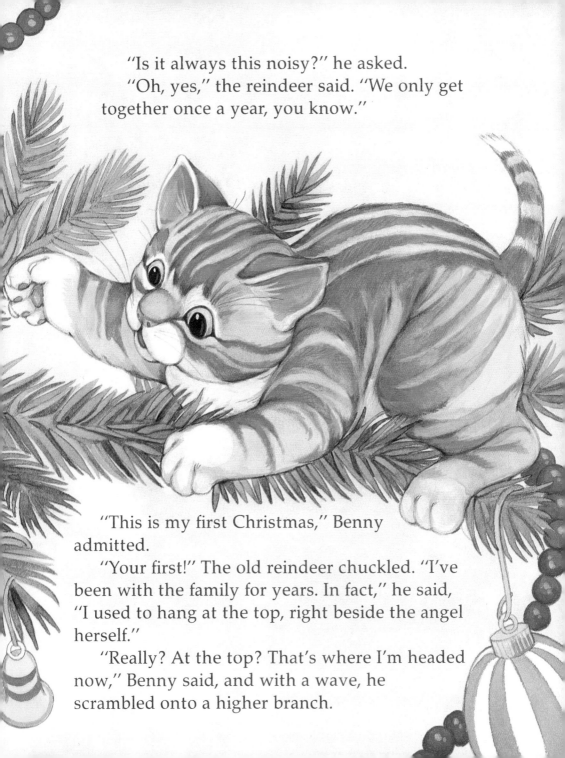

"Is it always this noisy?" he asked.

"Oh, yes," the reindeer said. "We only get together once a year, you know."

"This is my first Christmas," Benny admitted.

"Your first!" The old reindeer chuckled. "I've been with the family for years. In fact," he said, "I used to hang at the top, right beside the angel herself."

"Really? At the top? That's where I'm headed now," Benny said, and with a wave, he scrambled onto a higher branch.

Up Benny climbed, past silver flutes and tiny drums.

Miniature skaters called to one another,

and old-fashioned clothespin ladies gossiped on their boughs.

Suddenly a familiar squeal caught his attention. A velvet mouse peeked out of a red stocking. Curious, Benny approached. The mouse ducked out of sight.

"Go away!" the mouse cried.

"Don't worry," Benny said reassuringly. "I never hunt velvet mice. Besides, I'm on my way to the top of the tree."

The mouse cautiously rose from his stocking and regarded Benny with interest. "That's very unusual," the mouse said, "and possibly risky."

"Cats thrive on risks," Benny scoffed. "Just the other day I jumped right from the kitchen counter to the table. And I was carrying a piece of bacon at the same time."

"I'm sure you're good," the mouse said. "But there are sharp needles and shaky branches, not to mention the soldiers who guard the top of the tree. You'll never get past them!"

"I'll keep that in mind." Benny smiled. "How about a game of tag on my way back?"

"No, thanks!" the mouse cried and quickly disappeared into his stocking.

Benny climbed higher. He stopped beside a red sled to admire a beautiful bird. She was perched before a tiny music stand, and her long, iridescent tail swept to the branch below.

"Why, it's a cat!" the bird cried. "However did you get up here?"

"I climbed," said Benny proudly.

"Such bravery! Your reward shall be a song! Everyone tells me I have a very fine voice."

Benny glanced up. Was that the lacy hem of the angel's skirt up ahead? "No," he said. "I can't stay."

Benny reached the next branch. Chinese ladies whispered behind their fans. One pointed at something over Benny's shoulder.

Before he could turn, Benny heard a shout.

"Halt! Who goes there?" The soldiers!
Their leader advanced and stood before Benny.

"I'm Benny the cat," Benny answered in his
most charming voice. "I've come to see the top of
the tree."

"No cats in this tree!" the leader said firmly.
"Go back!"

"But I'd love to see the angel," Benny said,
smiling pleasantly. "I'll just be a minute."

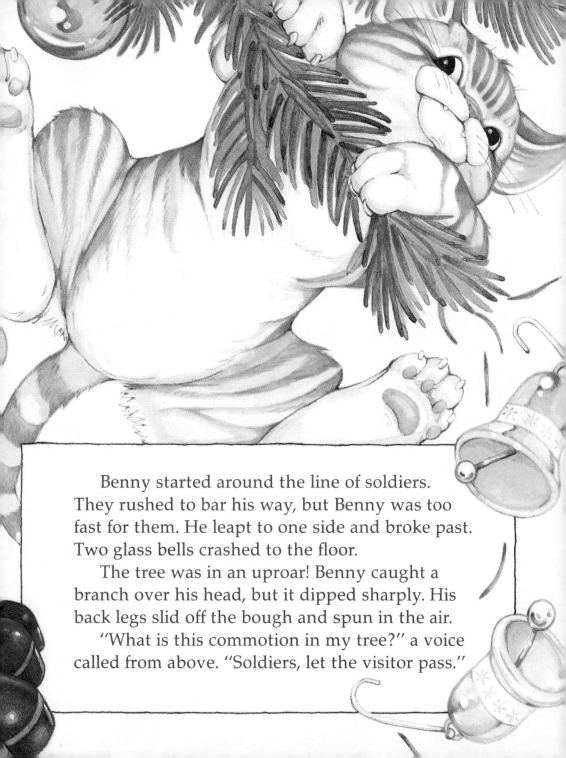

Benny started around the line of soldiers. They rushed to bar his way, but Benny was too fast for them. He leapt to one side and broke past. Two glass bells crashed to the floor.

The tree was in an uproar! Benny caught a branch over his head, but it dipped sharply. His back legs slid off the bough and spun in the air.

"What is this commotion in my tree?" a voice called from above. "Soldiers, let the visitor pass."

The soldiers withdrew. Benny regained his footing and made his way to the topmost branch.

The angel stood on her fluffy cloud. Benny had never seen such a beautiful creature. She wore a long gown of satin and lace, and she had two graceful silk wings.

"Benny, what is this disturbance?" she asked.

"I was just out for a climb," Benny explained. "How do you know my name?"

"I am the guardian angel. I watch and protect all the household at Christmastime."

"Even me?"

"Oh, yes. Especially you!"

Benny studied a paw while he thought this over.

"Benny, cats do not belong in Christmas trees," the angel continued, more gently now. "Didn't your family tell you that?"

"I guess so."

The angel sighed. "Well, you must leave now. How are you going to get down?"

Down! Benny hadn't thought of that. He gazed over the edge of the branch. It was a long way to the floor.

Benny remembered a time last summer when he'd been rescued from the garage roof with a ladder. Of course, he was just a kitten then.

"Actually, my specialty is the climb up," Benny said, looking back at the angel. "Usually I just wrap my paws around the trunk and scoot down backward."

The angel smiled. "I think that might be disastrous for the tree. Any other ideas?"

"I don't suppose you have a ladder?" Benny asked hopefully.

The angel shook her head.

"Well, then," Benny announced, "I'll just have to go down the way I came up." Benny jumped to a lower branch. But the branch drooped when he landed, and then the entire tree began to sway.

"Halt!" the soldiers shouted.

"My music stand!" chirped the bird.

"I knew this would happen!" the mouse squealed.

"Benny, come back!" the angel called. "We must get you down another way. Soldiers, please bring me the red sled, four branches down."

Benny heard a rustling. In a moment, two soldiers appeared, carrying the brightly painted sled. Somehow, the sled seemed larger here, on the highest bough. When the angel said, "Step on," Benny found that he just fit, although he had to tuck his tail in.

"This is great!" Benny cried. "Can I do loops?"

"No loops," the angel said. "Behave yourself. I'll be watching."

The angel reached down and stroked Benny's head. Her touch was as soft as the velvet inside the old violin case where Benny had once fallen asleep.

Then she smiled. "Are you ready? I'll push you."

The sled sailed off the tree. "Good-bye! Good-bye!" Benny called. Down he glided in the moonlight, past wooden soldiers who saluted and Chinese ladies who waved their fans, past rocking horses and the iridescent bird. He could not resist swooping close to the velvet mouse, who ducked into his red stocking as Benny passed by.

At last Benny landed on the carpet, just below the fuzzy reindeer.

"That was the best climb ever," he purred as he stretched and headed for his basket.

On Christmas morning the family found Benny unusually sweet and well behaved. And he didn't jump on a single countertop until sometime after New Year's Day.